D1514293

KN

'lease renew or return items by the date
ɔwn on your receipt

ˈw.hertfordshire.gov.uk/libraries

ɘwals and enquiries: 0300 123 4049

hone for hearing or 0300 123 4041
h impaired users:

Hertfordshire

525 998 22 7

With special thanks to Tom Easton

ORCHARD BOOKS
Carmelite House
50 Victoria Embankment
London EC4Y 0DZ

This edition published by Orchard Books in 2017

A CIP catalogue record for this book is available
from the British Library.

ISBN 978 1 40834 637 2

1 3 5 7 9 10 8 6 4 2

Printed in China

Orchard Books
An imprint of Hachette Children's Group
Part of The Watts Publishing Group Limited
An Hachette UK Company
www.hachette.co.uk

TRANSFORMERS
ROBOTS IN DISGUISE

BUMBLEBEE
THE BOSS

ORCHARD

ROLL OUT!

BUMBLEBEE

SIDESWIPE

GRIMLOCK

STRONGARM

FIXIT

CONTENTS

Part One:

A GOOD LEADER

Chapter One

MIRROR, MIRROR

Bumblebee and Fixit were in a scrapyard, looking at a map.

"This map shows where the stasis pods are," Bumblebee explained. "In each pod is a bad robot called a Decepticon."

"Look!" Fixit said. "The shape of the map looks a bit like a bad robot's face."

"We have to find the Decepticons," Bumblebee said.

Strongarm and Sideswipe arrived. They were arguing, like they always did.

"Get your finger out of my audio socket!" Strongarm said. She pushed Sideswipe away and he fell over. Grimlock laughed.

"Come on, team," Bumblebee cried. "Stop fighting. We have important work to do." But the others ignored him.

"They just won't listen to me," Bumblebee sighed sadly.

"No one listens to me and everyone listens to Optimus Prime." Optimus Prime was the leader of the Autobots. He was Bumblebee's hero.

"Why don't you ask him what to do?" Fixit suggested.

Bumblebee walked over to some old mirrors. Optimus was trapped in a place called the Realm of the Primes and the only way to talk to him was through a reflection. Bumblebee wasn't sure if this was going to work, but he tried anyway.

"How can I make everyone
listen to me?" he asked. But
Optimus didn't reply. All
Bumblebee could see was his
own reflection.

Just then, there was a huge
roar and a groaning sound.

Sideswipe had climbed up a
tower of junk and was standing
right at the top. The tower
creaked. It was going to fall.
And Strongarm was standing
right underneath it!

Chapter Two

A BAD ROBOT

Bumblebee leapt into the air and changed into a fast yellow sports car. He landed on the

dusty ground and raced towards the tower, pushing Strongarm out of danger. But with a creak and a crunch, the tower of rubbish fell on top of Bumblebee!

Bumblebee was under a pile of rubbish. He pushed an old pinball table away. It flashed and played a tune.

As Bumblebee got up, all the Autobots laughed.

I need to be more like Optimus Prime. No one laughs at him, Bumblebee thought. He threw off the junk and stood tall.

Then he tried to talk in a deep voice like his hero.

"Autobots! We have to track down the escaped Decepticons. If we don't stop them, they'll smash up the city."

Sideswipe, Strongarm and Grimlock stopped talking and looked at him. *They're listening to me,* thought Bumblebee. *It's working!*

"Optimus Prime said I was in charge," Bumblebee went on.

"So you need to follow me and do what I say."

There was a pause. Then Grimlock and Strongarm burst out laughing. "Why are you talking in a funny voice?" Sideswipe asked.

Bumblebee felt sad. *I'll never be a good leader like Optimus Prime,* he thought.

"There's something you need to see," Fixit called. "Turn on the news."

The Autobots' human friend, Denny, turned on an old TV in the workshop. A news report showed a picture of a large metal box. "The strange object has been taken to the City Museum to be studied," the reporter said.

"I know what it is," Bumblebee said. "That's a stasis pod. There's a Decepticon inside. We have to stop him from escaping!"

Chapter Three

AUTOBOTS ROLL OUT!

"We need to find a way into that museum," said Bumblebee. "But how?"

"I think I know a way," said Denny. "I'll disguise myself as an explorer. I can distract the guard. Then you can all sneak into the museum."

Bumblebee thought for a moment. "I think that might work," he said.

"I'm coming too," Denny's son, Russell, said.

"It will be dangerous," Denny said, stroking his beard. "But if you follow me then I guess you can come. You have to do what I say, OK?" He put an explorer's hat on Russell. It slipped down over his eyes.

"How can I follow you if I can't even see you?" Russell said with a laugh.

"Speaking of disguises," Bumblebee said, "we'd better cover Grimlock so he doesn't attract too much attention."

Grimlock was a Dinobot. He could change from a robot into a huge T-Rex, but he couldn't turn into a car like the other robots.

"Come on, everyone, let's go!" Bumblebee said. The Autobots changed into cars.

They roared out of the scrapyard in a huge cloud of dust. First Bumblebee, as a yellow car, then Sideswipe. He was a super-fast red sports car. Behind them came Strongarm, looking like a police car.

Strongarm was pulling Grimlock
on a covered trailer.

   The Autobots raced into
action!

Part Two:

THE MUSEUM
PLAN

Chapter Four

COWBOYS AND ROBOTS

The Autobots arrived at the back door of the museum with a screech of tyres. Strongarm changed back into a robot.

"Help me get this cover off Grimlock," she called. But a gust of wind blew the cover over her and Grimlock!

"Help!" Strongarm shouted.

"Get off!" Grimlock roared.

Strongarm and Grimlock
struggled with the cover.
Sideswipe laughed.

"Stop messing about, guys,"
Bumblebee said, crossly. "This
is serious!"

Denny and Russell went
into the museum, dressed as
explorers.

"We're closed," said the
guard.

"I know," Denny said. "My
name is Professor … err, Benny.
And this is my assistant … he's
called … err …"

"I'm called Mr McPlank," said
Russell.

"I have just returned from my
latest trip to the jungle," Denny
continued, "and I am looking for
a museum to give some treasure
to. Can we look around?"

"OK!" the museum guard replied, eagerly.

Inside the museum, Denny and Russell went to the back door and opened it. All the Autobots came in.

"Look at this!" Bumblebee said. "A display about cowboys."

"I'd love to be a cowboy," said Sideswipe. "No one would tell me what to do."

"Actually," Bumblebee replied, "*real* cowboys always worked together as a team to round up their cattle." Bumblebee tried to sound like Optimus Prime again. But before he'd finished talking, the other Autobots drove off. Bumblebee sighed, feeling sad that no one was listening to him.

"You could learn something about being a team from me and Russell," Denny said. "Isn't that right, Russell? Russell?"

But Russell had disappeared as well.

Chapter Five

A BIG, BAD BUFFALO

Russell walked alone down a dark corridor, pretending to be Mr McPlank, the famous explorer. He came into a big room and gasped as he saw a huge stasis pod. Russell crept closer. *Is there a Decepticon inside?* he thought.

Suddenly, with a loud roar, the stasis pod blasted open.

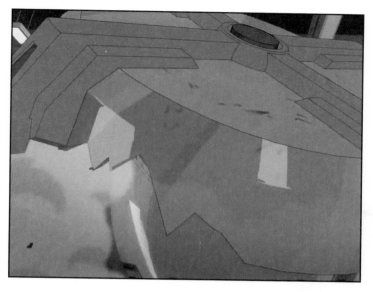

A piece of metal flew right towards Russell. It was going to hit him!

Russell dived for cover. The sharp piece of metal only just missed his head.

"That was close," he said.

Then he looked up to see ...
A huge buffalo!

But it wasn't an ordinary
buffalo, it was a bad robot
in disguise. It was a type of
Decepticon called a Buffaloid!

The Buffaloid roared and punched a machine, smashing it into tiny pieces. "My name is Terrashock," the Buffaloid said. "Someone put me in a tiny box! NOBODY puts Terrashock in a tiny box!" He roared again and smashed what was left of the stasis pod.

Just then, Sideswipe arrived. "Are you OK?" he asked Russell. Russell nodded.

"Did you put me in the box?" Terrashock asked Sideswipe.

"No," Sideswipe replied.

"Do you think I'm stupid?" Terrashock asked.

"Is that a trick question?" Sideswipe replied.

Terrashock roared in anger. Suddenly he charged at the door ... right towards Russell!

Chapter Six

OUT OF MY WAY!

As the huge Buffaloid rushed at him, Russell was scared. "Wait, wait …" he said. Terrashock ran forward, but luckily he missed Russell. He smashed through the wall instead. Terrashock stopped in the corridor and looked around.

"He looks confused," Sideswipe said. "I don't think he's very smart."

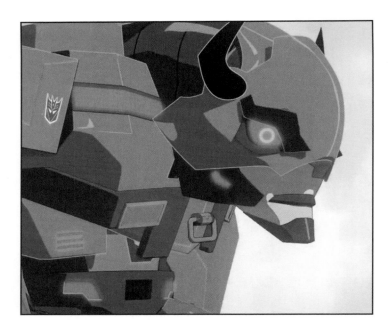

Terrashock rushed off down the corridor. "If anyone gets in my way they're going to get smashed!" he roared.

Sideswipe changed into a car. "Get in," he said to Russell.

"Where are we going?" Russell asked.

"We are going to get in his way," Sideswipe replied. He radioed the other Autobots. "A Decepticon has escaped," he told them.

"His name is Terrashock," Russell added. "He has a big head, but a small brain!"

"Don't try to fight him on your own," Bumblebee said. "If you see him, call the rest of us. We work as a team."

"Yeah, yeah," Sideswipe said.

He turned off his radio.

Terrashock thundered into the cowboy display room and skidded to a stop as he saw a model of a buffalo. It looked just like him! "Hello!" he said to the model. But the buffalo model didn't reply.

Terrashock snorted in fury and charged into the display, crushing the buffalo model. Strongarm walked in.

"I saw that!" she cried. "You are under arrest for damaging museum property."

But Terrashock just turned
and charged into Strongarm,
knocking her over.

"I guess this means you're
not going to come quietly,"
Strongarm sighed, as Terrashock
ran away.

Next Terrashock ran into
a big, dark room. Stars shone

across the ceiling. Terrashock cried out in fear.

Just then, Grimlock rushed into the room and charged at the Buffaloid, who turned and charged back. Their hard heads met with a *CRUNCH*!

Grimlock was thrown up into the air. Terrashock hit the wall with a *BOOM* as Sideswipe came in.

He's really dumb, thought Sideswipe. He leapt on to Terrashock's back like a rodeo rider. Terrashock roared and bucked. Sideswipe lost his grip and was thrown off. He landed on the floor with a *THUMP.*

Sideswipe moaned as Terrashock rushed off again.

Could anyone stop this super-strong Decepticon?

Part Three:
BE YOURSELF

Chapter Seven

BE YOURSELF

Bumblebee was walking through the museum, looking for the others. He felt sad. "I just don't know how I'm ever going to get my team to listen to me," he said to Denny. "I wish I was more like Optimus Prime."

Suddenly he heard a sound. Optimus Prime's face had appeared in a pane of glass.

"Optimus!" Bumblebee cried.

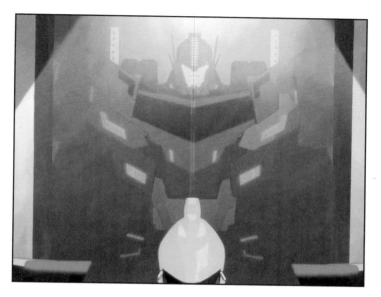

"We don't have long,"
Optimus said. "Tell me what is
happening."

"We found an escaped
Decepticon," Bumblebee said.

"Did you catch it and put it in
the stasis pod?" Optimus asked.

"We tried … but we failed," Bumblebee explained, sadly. "I'm not very good at being a leader, even when I try to be like you."

"But you aren't me …" Optimus Prime began. Just then the sound faded away.

"I know," Bumblebee said. "I'm sorry. I've let you down."

"That's not what I mean," Optimus Prime said as the sound came back. "What I'm saying is ..." But before he could finish talking, the picture and sound faded away again. Optimus Prime was gone.

"Maybe I should quit as leader of the Autobots," Bumblebee said, with a sigh.

"You can be a great leader," Denny told him.

Bumblebee shook his head.

"You heard Optimus," Bumblebee said, "I am not like him ..."

"Maybe you should stop trying to be like him, and just be yourself," said Denny.

Bumblebee thought about what Denny had said, but before he could reply, there was a huge crash as an enormous robot burst through the door, roaring in fury.

"I think we have found our escaped Decepticon," said Denny.

Chapter Eight

A RUBBISH ROBOT

"Finally!" Terrashock roared. "I'm outside." As Bumblebee and Denny watched in amazement, Terrashock changed into a huge dustbin lorry. He raced off towards the city.

Bumblebee turned on his radio. "Autobots, come here." he said. Strongarm, Sideswipe and Grimlock came racing up, along with Russell.

"OK, team," Bumblebee said. "We have to catch that Buffaloid before he gets to the city. He could do a lot of damage there."

"But he is so big," Strongarm said.

"And so fast," added Sideswipe.

"And his head is so hard," groaned Grimlock. "How can we stop him?"

"Easy," Bumblebee said. "We'll be like cowboys."

"Cowboys?" Grimlock said, looking confused.

"Didn't you learn anything in the museum today?" Bumblebee asked, shaking his head. "Cowboys always work as a team. Autobots, let's roll out!"

The Autobots quickly changed back into their car forms. Their tyres screeched as they raced off after the bad robot.

Terrashock was fast, but the Autobots were faster.

"We need to show him who's boss," Bumblebee radioed to the others as they came up beside the lorry.

But just then, Terrashock swerved sharply towards Bumblebee. The massive lorry would crush him like he was a piece of rubbish!

Chapter Nine

Thinking quickly, Bumblebee turned to the left and drove up the grassy bank at the side of the road.

That was close!

"Come on, cowboys," Bumblebee cried, coming back down the slope on to the highway. "Let's catch him."

"Yee-haa!" cried Strongarm. They got closer to Terrashock, who changed back into a Buffaloid and charged down the road. The Autobots worked together. Bumblebee drove out in front of Terrashock.

Terrashock roared and turned quickly, crashing into a wall. Grimlock jumped on top of the Buffaloid, pinning him down.

"You caught him!" Strongarm shouted.

"No," Bumblebee replied. "*We* caught him, because we worked as a team."

"And you were the boss," Denny said to Bumblebee. "All the others started listening to you when you stopped trying to be like Optimus Prime and started to be yourself."

The traffic had stopped. People were staring in amazement at the robots. Thinking quickly, Russell grabbed a megaphone. "There's nothing to see here, folks," he said, his voice crackling and booming.

"We're just making a film."

"You know what? I think we all make a great team," Bumblebee said.

"And if Optimus Prime was here," Denny said with a grin, "I think he might just agree."

The Autobots started to go home. Another bad robot had been caught and another mission was complete.

The End

WELL DONE!

You've finished this adventure!